EARLY FLUENT

D0456729

Rafi and Rosi Pirates!

Lulu Delacre

Children's Book Press, *an imprint of* Lee & Low Books Inc.
New York

To big brothers and their little sisters

Acknowledgments
Grateful thanks to Olga Jiménez de Wagenheim, Professor Emerita in History, Rutgers University, and Dr. Camilla Stevens, Associate Professor of Latino and Caribbean Studies/Spanish, Rutgers University, for reviewing the informational material in the "Did You Know About . . ." section of the book.

Author's Sources
Brau, Salvador. *Historia de Puerto Rico*, Ediciones Borinquen, Editorial Coquí: San Juan, Puerto Rico, 1966.
Coll y Toste, Cayetano. *Leyendas y Tradiciones Puertorriqueñas*. Editorial Cultural, Inc.: Río Piedras, Puerto Rico, 1975.
Fortines de Puerto Rico. http://www.prfrogui.com/home/fortines.htm.
"History of the Spanish Doubloon." Northwest Territorial Mint. https://store.nwtmint.com/info/doubloon/.
"Maps." San Juan National Historic Site, Puerto Rico. National Park Service. https://www.nps.gov/saju/planyourvisit/maps.htm.
Negrón Hernández Jr., Luis R. "Roberto Cofresí: El pirata caborrojeño." PReb.com. http://www.preb.com/biog/hcofresi.htm.
"Pirate Money." Pirates of the Caribbean in Fact and Fiction. http://pirates.hegewisch.net/money.html.
"San Juan National Historic Site, Puerto Rico." National Park Service. https://www.nps.gov/nr/travel/american_latino_heritage/san_juan_national_historic_site.html.
San Juan National Historic Site, Puerto Rico. National Park Service informational brochures: 2004, 2006, 2016.
"Spanish Colonial History." Wayback Machine Internet Archive. https://web.archive.org/web/20011030171948/http://americanhistory si edu/vidal/history htm

Children's Book Press, an imprint of LEE & LOW BOOKS INC.,
95 Madison Avenue, New York, NY 10016, leeandlow.com
Book design by David and Susan Neuhaus/NeuStudio
Book production by The Kids at Our House
The text is set in Times Regular. The illustrations are rendered in watercolor and colored pencil on Arches watercolor paper.
Manufactured in China by Imago, August 2017
Printed on paper from responsible sources
(HC) 10 9 8 7 6 5 4 3 2 1
(PBK) 10 9 8 7 6 5 4 3 2 1
First Edition
Library of Congress Cataloging-in-Publication Data
Names: Delacre, Lulu, author, illustrator.
Title: Rafi and Rosi : pirates! / Lulu Delacre. Other titles: Pirates!
Description: First edition. | New York : Children's Book Press, an imprint of Lee & Low Books Inc., [2017] | Series: Dive into reading | Summary: "Rafi and Rosi, two curious tree frogs, explore Puerto Rico's El Morro Fort, where they pretend to be pirates in battle, find pirate treasure, and discover a haunted sentry box"—Provided by publisher. Includes glossary and facts about the places and events. | Includes bibliographical references.
Identifiers: LCCN 2017008779 |
ISBN 9780892393817 (hardcover : alk. paper) | ISBN 9780892393831 (pbk. : alk. paper)
Subjects: | CYAC: Tree frogs—Fiction. | Frogs—Fiction. | Brothers and sisters—Fiction. | Pirates—Fiction. | San Juan National Historic Site (San Juan, P.R.) | Puerto Rico—Fiction.
Classification: LCC PZ7.D3696 Rcp 2017 | DDC [E]—dc23
LC record available at https://lccn.loc.gov/2017008779

Contents

Glossary

ahorita (ah-oh-REE-tah): A Puerto Rican way of saying "later."

¡Ay, caramba! (EYE, kah-RAHM-bah): Oh, goodness gracious! Used to express an emotion such as pain, disappointment, or anger.

bandanna: A large, colorful cloth used as a head covering or worn around the neck.

Cofresí (coh-freh-SEE): Puerto Rico's most famous pirate. He lived from 1791 to 1825.

coquí (coh-KEE): A tiny tree frog found in Puerto Rico that is named after its song.

Denmark: A country in northern Europe.

doubloon: An old gold coin from Spain or Spanish America.

El Morro (ehl MOH-rroh): A four-hundred-year-old fort that guards the entrance to San Juan harbor.

gracias (GRAH-see-ahs): Thank you.

hola (OH-lah): Hello.

morro (MOH-rroh): High, rocky area that sticks out into the sea.

Old San Juan (sahn HWAN): The oldest settled area of the island of Puerto Rico.

piece of eight: An old silver coin from Spain.

San Juan Bay (sahn HWAN): The body of water next to Old San Juan.

sentry box: A small shelter in which a lookout guard stands.

sí (see): Yes.

Spain: A country in western Europe.

Tía (TEE-ah): Aunt.

4

Pirate Battle

"Aha!" said Rafi Coquí,

closing his book.

He jumped up to look over the balcony

of Tía Ana's house in Old San Juan.

"What?" asked his little sister, Rosi.

She had just finished decorating

her new kite.

"Follow me," said Rafi.

He picked up his pirate hat,

his pirate flag, his fake sword,

two long sticks,

and a tube of Rosi's glitter.

He had a plan.

"Help me fly my kite," said Rosi.

"*Ahorita*," said Rafi. "Later."

Rafi ran out of Tía Ana's house
and all the way to El Morro fort.
Rosi trailed behind.
Entry to the fort was free today.
Rafi got to the very top of the fort
and climbed onto a pile
of cannonballs.

"Look at the ocean," said Rafi.

"That's where Pirate Cofresí

held a big battle."

Rosi rolled her eyes.

"I want to fly my kite," she said.

"But," said Rafi,

"Pirate Cofresí was—"

"I don't care about

pirates," said Rosi.

Rosi began to leave.

Rafi spoke in a big, booming voice.

"Pirate Cofresí was the grandfather

of our great-grandpa."

Rosi turned around.

"Great-grandpa's grandpa?" she asked.

"*Sí*," said Rafi. "Yes.

Tell the others to come listen."

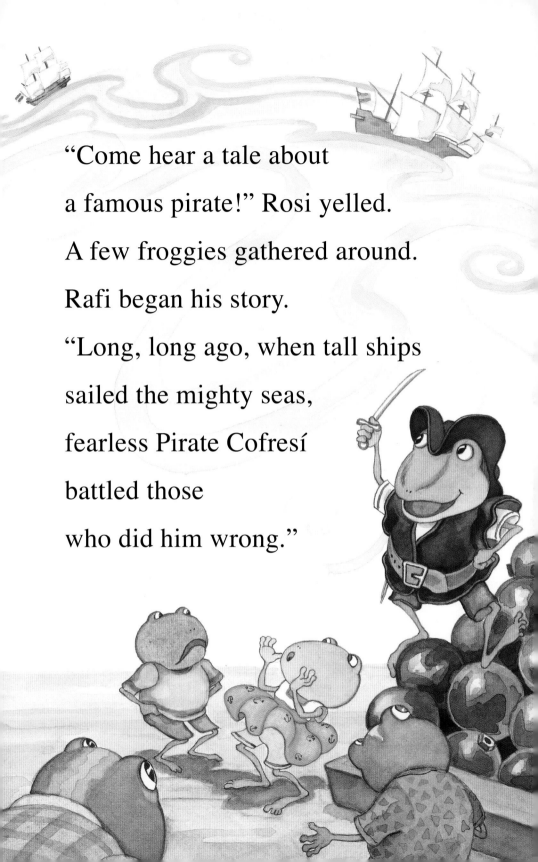

"Come hear a tale about
a famous pirate!" Rosi yelled.
A few froggies gathered around.
Rafi began his story.
"Long, long ago, when tall ships
sailed the mighty seas,
fearless Pirate Cofresí
battled those
who did him wrong."

The crowd grew and grew.

Rafi grabbed his long sticks

and tossed them in the air.

Two froggies caught them

and joined Rafi

in a make-believe pirate battle.

The froggies made their T-shirts

into pirate bandannas

to wrap around their heads.

Sticks became daggers and swords.

Rafi gave his pirate flag to Rosi.

She waved it back and forth.

"I see an enemy ship!" Rosi said.

"It's from Denmark," said Rafi.

"Let's climb on board
and look for silver and gold!
We'll take all the loot with us."

The pirates jumped

from the pile of cannonballs

to the cannon,

and from the cannon

back to the pile of cannonballs.

Rosi watched and listened.

She heard the seagulls' calls.

She heard the pirates' grunts.

The battle looked so real.

Rosi could almost see

Pirate Cofresí's tall ship.

From deep within this battle

Rafi threw his hat to Rosi.

"Grab it!" he yelled.

Rosi dropped the flag

to catch the hat.

"What should we do

with all the loot?" Rafi asked.

"Shall we give some to the poor?"

"Yes!" replied Rosi.

"Yes!" agreed the other pirates.

Rafi climbed onto the cannonballs.

"Pirate Cofresí gave away

half his loot," he said,

showering the crowd with glitter.

The pirates clapped and cheered.

"He took from the rich," said Rafi.

"And gave to the poor!"

shouted Rosi.

Above the noise of the crowd

a sharp whistle blew.

Rafi and Rosi saw

an angry guard

headed their way.

The guard blew the whistle

again and again.

Pirates leaped

off the cannonballs

and jumped off the cannon.

They scattered everywhere

until Pirate Cofresí's tall ship

vanished right before Rosi's eyes.

"What happened?"

Rosi asked,

still holding

Rafi's hat.

Two froggies dropped money

into the hat.

"Great tale," they said.

"*Gracias*," said Rafi. "Thank you."

He scooped up half the coins.

"Here, Rosi," he said. "For you."

"Let's fly your kite now," Rafi said,

just before the guard reached them.

"*¡Sí!*" said Rosi. "Yes!"

And off they ran—out of the fort

and into the open field.

24

Hidden
Treasure

"Let's go back and explore the fort,"
Rafi said after lunch.

"What else can we see?" Rosi asked.

Rafi looked at his map of El Morro.

"Lots more cannons," said Rafi.

"And a kitchen."

"A kitchen in a fort?"
asked Rosi.

"Of course," said Rafi.

"The Spanish soldiers
guarding the city
had to cook food to eat."

Rosi skipped all the way to the fort.

Rafi trailed behind,
checking his map.

"We have to go that way," Rafi said,

pointing to some steps.

"I want to look at the ships," said Rosi.

She ran to a lookout point

over San Juan Bay.

Rosi closed her eyes

and breathed in the salty air.

When she opened her eyes again

she saw a butterfly.

She tried to touch it, but it flew away.

Rosi followed the butterfly
down to the very bottom of the fort.
The butterfly landed on a brick
inside a room built out of stone.
Rosi tiptoed in.
A ray of sunlight shone on the brick.
Something sparkled.

"Rosi, you found the kitchen!"
said Rafi, walking into the room.
"There's something hidden
in there," said Rosi.

"Really?" said Rafi. "Let's check."

Rafi grabbed a stick.

He moved the brick a tiny bit.

Rosi slipped her hand

into the space under the brick.

"I feel something," said Rosi.

"It's clinking!"

Rafi and Rosi looked at each other.

"I'll loosen the brick," said Rafi.

He tugged and tugged

until the brick fell to the ground.

A soft pouch fell too.

"WOW!" Rosi and Rafi shouted.

Gold and silver coins

spilled across the floor.

"Is this real money?" asked Rosi.

"It's, it's . . . it's *pirate* money!"

Rafi said. "See the lions

and the towers on the coins?

They stand for the king

and queen of Spain."

"Pirates used Spanish coins?"
asked Rosi.

"They stole them from
the tall ships," said Rafi.

Rosi felt the roughness
of the coins with her finger.

"It looks like we found
a pirate's treasure,"
she said.

"What will we do with the money?"

asked Rosi.

Rafi sighed. "We can't keep it," he said.

"Why not? We found it," said Rosi.

"If these old Spanish coins are real,

we have to turn them in

to the museum," said Rafi.

"Oh," said Rosi.

"Can't you keep just one coin
for your collection of pirate stuff?"

"I don't know," said Rafi.

"Let's show the coins
to the museum expert."

"Maybe the expert will let you
keep one," said Rosi.

Rafi and Rosi ran all the way up
to the museum and found the expert.
"*Hola*," said Rosi. "Hello.
We found a treasure hidden
in the kitchen of the fort.
My brother says it's pirate money."
"Is that so?" said the expert.
"Show her, Rafi," said Rosi.

Rafi emptied the pouch.

"Oh, my!" said the expert, examining each coin.

"These *are* real," she said.

"They are Spanish gold doubloons and silver pieces of eight."

"See?" said Rosi.

"I can't believe it," said Rafi.

"We found real pirate money."

"Could my brother
keep one?" begged Rosi.
"I'm afraid not,"
said the expert.
"The coins belong in the museum."
"I thought so," said Rafi.
Rosi squeezed Rafi's hand.
His hand was smooth,
not rough like the coins.
"Hmm . . . ," Rosi said. "Wait!"

Rosi turned around. "Could we make rubbings of the coins?" Rosi asked the expert.

"I don't see why not," she replied, giving Rosi some colored pencils.

"Thank you! *¡Gracias!* Thank you!" Rosi said, jumping up and down.

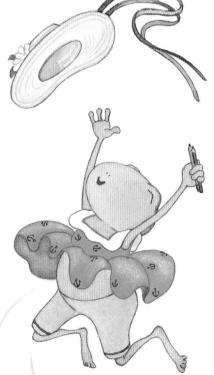

Rafi and Rosi rubbed their pencils
over each gold and silver coin
until every little detail showed.

They could keep

these coins

forever.

Haunted
Sentry Box

It was late in the afternoon,
and Rafi and Rosi
were still at El Morro Fort.
They were playing hide-and-seek.
"I found you!" yelled Rosi.
"Now it's my turn to hide."
"We need to go back to Tía Ana's,"
said Rafi.

"One last time," begged Rosi.

"Pleeease."

"Okay," Rafi said.

He closed his eyes

and started to count.

"One, two, three . . ."

Rosi looked around and found

the perfect place to hide.

Rafi searched for Rosi.

He looked behind the cannonballs
and under cannons.

He went down the ramp
and checked the museum.

Far away he saw a sentry box.

Spanish soldiers once stood
inside it to guard the fort.

Rafi ran to the sentry box.

"Here you are!" Rafi said.

"You are just in time," said Rosi.

"Lift me up, please.

I heard strange noises

outside the window."

When Rafi lifted Rosi up

he saw deep grooves

in the windowsill.

He thought of something.

"Maybe the noises are coming

from the giant sea monster," said Rafi.

"What giant sea monster?" asked Rosi.

"The one that did this," said Rafi,

pointing to the grooves.

"You're making that up!" yelled Rosi.

She was upset.

Rafi had tried to scare her.

So Rosi made up her own story.

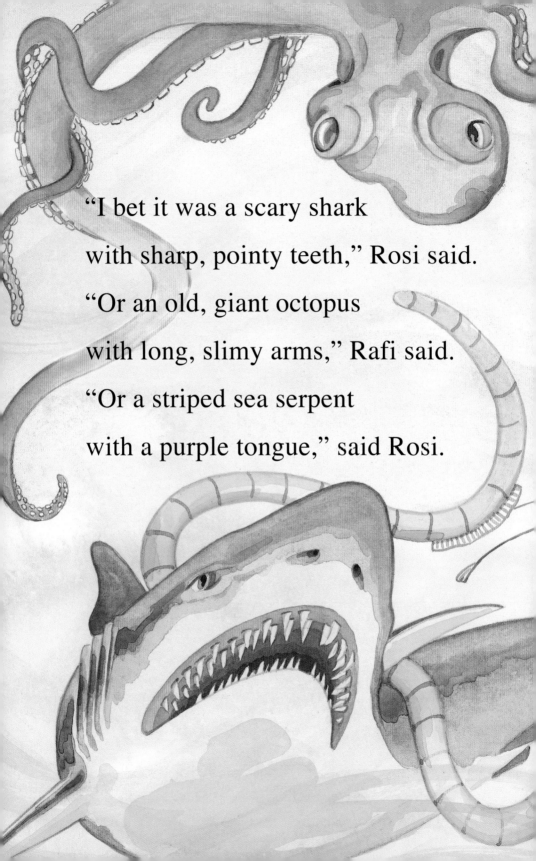

"I bet it was a scary shark
with sharp, pointy teeth," Rosi said.
"Or an old, giant octopus
with long, slimy arms," Rafi said.
"Or a striped sea serpent
with a purple tongue," said Rosi.

Rosi heard the noises again.

They sounded like sad squeaks.

"What is it?" she asked, worried.

Rafi ran to the other window.

"Who's there?" he shouted.

Shrill sounds rose up

from the darkness below.

Rafi was puzzled.

He checked his map of the fort.

"Oh, no," he said.

"We're in the haunted sentry box!"

"What?" said Rosi.

"It seems that long ago a guard

disappeared from here," said Rafi.

Rosi trembled a little.

She turned to look at Rafi's map.

The wind pulled the ribbons

of her hat out the window.

Then something tugged at the ribbons.

"*¡Ay, caramba!*" Rosi cried.

"Who's there?" Rafi called.

More shrill sounds rose up.

Then they heard a thump.

"I'm leaving!" Rosi screamed.

She fled out the door.

"Wait for me!" Rafi yelled.

Outside, Rosi started to cry.

"It's okay," said Rafi.

"We'll go to Tía Ana's house now."

"But my hat," sobbed Rosi.

"The monster got it."

Rafi looked at the haunted sentry box.

Then he looked at his little sister.

He took a big, long breath

before he walked back.

At the door he heard

the strange noises.

He went inside.

Rosi's hat hung
from the windowsill.
It wiggled now and then.
Rafi held his breath,
closed his eyes,
grabbed the hat,
and pulled hard.
He fell back onto the floor.
"Ouch!" he cried.

Frightened mice dangled

from the ribbons of the hat.

They scurried away,

vanishing into the cracks

in the walls of the sentry box.

Rafi snatched Rosi's hat

and raced back to her.

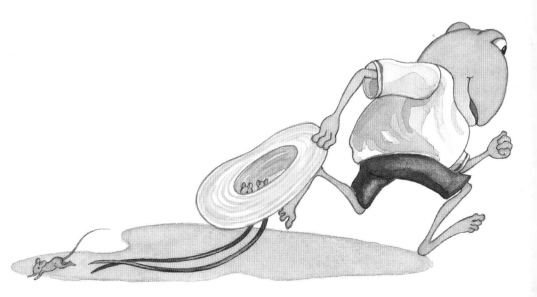

"The sentry box is only haunted by mice!" announced Rafi.

"Just mice?" Rosi said.

Then she started to giggle.

Rafi and Rosi
laughed and laughed
until their bellies hurt.

Did You Know About . . .

. . . El Morro Fort?

El Morro Fort, officially named Castillo de San Felipe del Morro, was started in 1539 by Spanish colonizers. The fort was named after King Philip II of Spain and the place where it is perched—on a *morro*, a high, rocky area that sticks out into the sea. The Spanish wanted to protect the entrance to San Juan Bay because Puerto Rico was the first major island that sailing ships met on their way to the Americas. Engineers spent almost two hundred fifty years building El Morro. It was completed in 1787 and is one of the three oldest and largest forts in the Caribbean.

The fort has been attacked many times throughout the centuries. In 1595, Sir Francis Drake, an English sea captain considered a pirate by the Spanish, led an attack with twenty-four tall ships. Gunners from El Morro shot a cannonball through the cabin of Drake's flagship. The following day the English fleet fled. The fort has also been attacked by the Dutch Republic and the United States. In 1898, El Morro suffered its last attack. It came from the US Navy during the Spanish-American War.

. . . Pirate Cofresí?

Roberto Cofresí was born in 1791 in Cabo Rojo, Puerto Rico. He was the son of a German nobleman and a Puerto Rican woman from a wealthy family. Cofresí's mother died when he was four, and his father died nine years later. Left on his own, Cofresí worked as a sailor. Other sailors eventually joined him, and they turned to piracy. Pirate Cofresí attacked Dutch, English, and United States ships in the Caribbean Sea. Since Cofresí interfered with international trade, many countries wanted to get rid of him. In March 1825, Spain, Denmark, and the United States joined together to ambush Cofresí at sea. The pirate fled to Puerto Rico, and the local government captured him on the southeastern shore of the island. They sent Pirate Cofresí to El Morro Fort, where he was imprisoned, tried, and sentenced to death. He was killed by a firing squad just three weeks after his capture.

Cofresí was the last pirate of the Caribbean. He is said to have stolen from the rich and given to the poor, sharing some of his spoils with the needy and elderly. Treasure hunters today still look for Cofresí's treasure, believed to be hidden on the coast of Cabo Rojo.

. . . Pirate Money?
Spanish gold doubloons and silver pieces of eight were widely used as money in international trade from the sixteenth century to the mid-nineteenth century. The Spanish explorers minted thousands

of coins from the tons of gold and silver they
took from Mexico and South America. The coins
were originally made by hand, and their value was
determined by their weight. A Spanish doubloon
was made of seven grams (a quarter ounce) of
fine gold. Workers sliced round bars of gold into
disks, stamped a design on each, and trimmed the disks
to achieve the right weights. One of the designs
on doubloons shows lions, towers, and a cross.
Lions and towers represent the coat of arms of
King Ferdinand and Queen Isabella of Spain, who
sent Christopher Columbus on his voyages. The
Jerusalem Cross, or Crusader's Cross, indicates
the close ties between the Spanish kingdom and the
Catholic religion.

Spanish sailing ships carried thousands of pounds
of gold and silver as they traveled from South
America and Central America to Europe. Pirates
in the Caribbean Sea were aware of this cargo and
constantly attacked the ships.

How to Make Coin Rubbings?

You will need: coins of any kind, sheets of thin
white paper, and a soft lead pencil or colored pencil.

1) Place the paper on a hard, flat surface.
2) Decide where you want the design of the coin
to appear on the paper. Place the coin on the hard
surface directly under that spot on the paper.

3) Hold the paper down firmly so neither the coin or the paper will move.

4) Using the side of the pencil point, rub back and forth on the paper over the coin underneath. Apply gentle, even pressure so the paper does not tear.

5) The design of the whole coin will appear on the paper as you continue rubbing.

6) Repeat with the other side of the coin or another coin on a different part of the paper. Continue until you have created an overall coin pattern on the paper.

   If you are careful, you will reveal tiny details on the coin that do not show up even in photographs!

. . . the Haunted Sentry Box Legend?

From the sixteenth century to the nineteenth century, Spanish soldiers stood guard along the coast to protect the city of Old San Juan. The soldiers themselves were protected by stone sentry boxes, structures built into the walls of forts. The haunted sentry box of the legend is located in Castillo de San Cristóbal, a fort to the east of El Morro. One night a handsome soldier standing guard duty vanished from his post. Troops searched for him but he was never found. Some said evil spirits took him away. Others believed the soldier fled with his girlfriend. The young girl to whom the soldier had sung love songs disappeared on the same night as the soldier.